CLIFF
The FAILED Troll

WARNING:
There Be Pirates
in This Book!

BARBARA DAVIS-PYLES

Illustrated by JUSTIN HILLGROVE

little bigfoot
an imprint of sasquatch books
seattle, wa

In class, the other students could sit still . . .

FOR *WEEKS.*

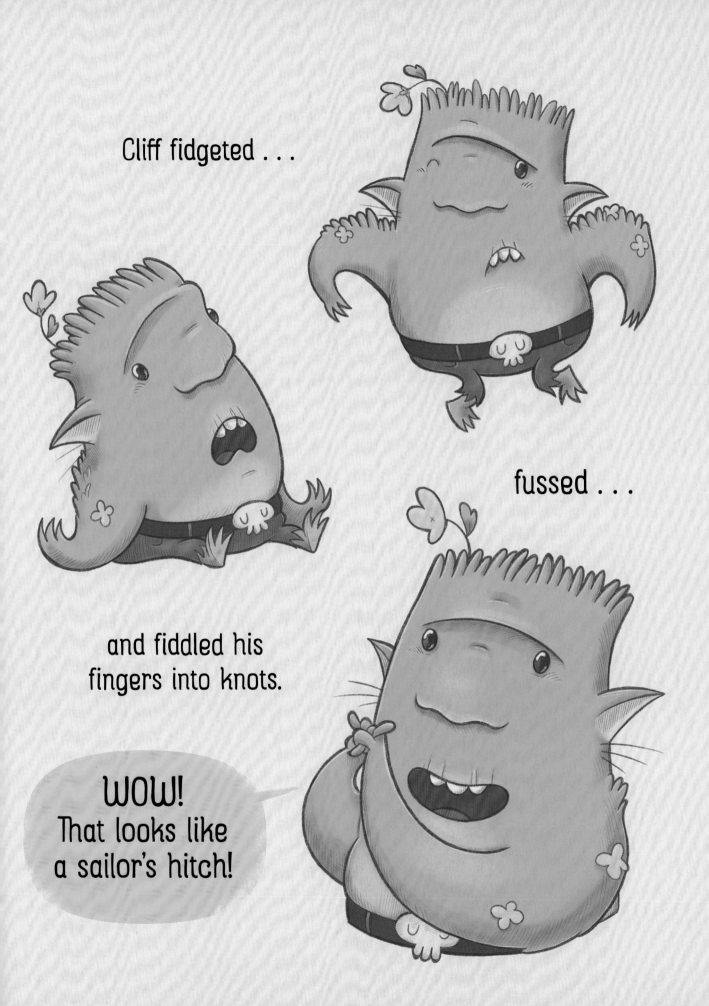

Cliff fidgeted . . .

fussed . . .

and fiddled his
fingers into knots.

WOW!
That looks like
a sailor's hitch!

Field trips were no better.
Whenever a wisp of wind tickled his ear whiskers,
Cliff couldn't keep from singing.

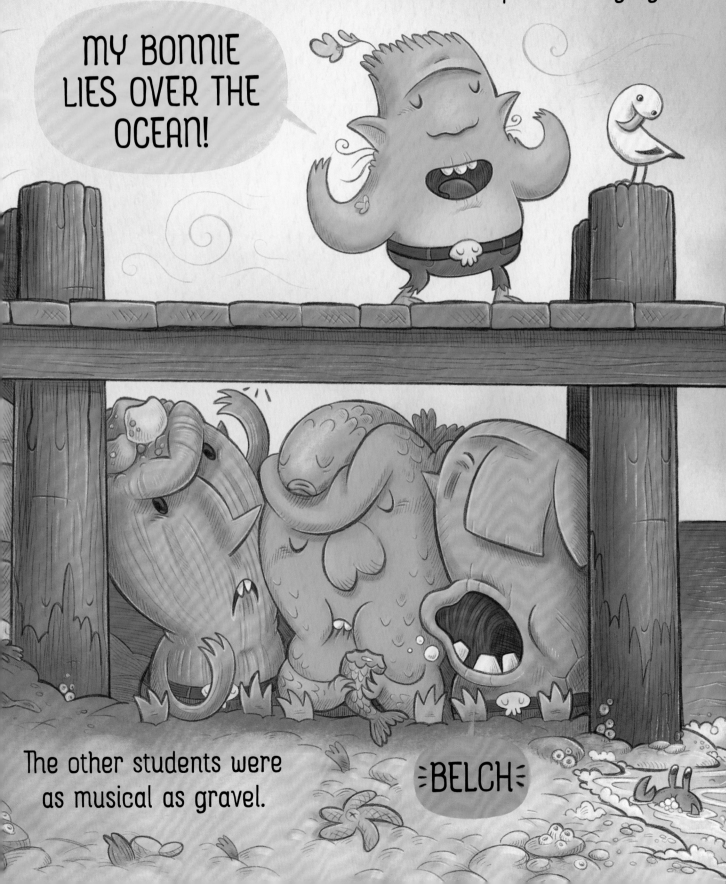

MY BONNIE
LIES OVER THE
OCEAN!

The other students were as musical as gravel.

BELCH

So, it was no surprise that Cliff's final report card looked like this:

He even got an **F** in Goat Gobbling.

I'm a vegetarian.

That's fine with me.
I don't want to be a troll anyway . . .
CLIFF
Bridge Building
F
F
F
F
Goat Gobbling

Cliff signed up for pirate school that very day,
packed his things, and set off for the Salish Sea.

He was so excited and in such a rush that he
didn't watch where he was going, so of course
he slipped on a banana . . .

I'm so sorry! Are you hurt?
No.
Then why are you crying?
I'm crying because I can't wear an eyepatch . . .
and that means I CAN'T BE A PIRATE!
WAAAH!

Cliff scooped up Polly and plopped her on his shoulder.

YAY!
I mean,
YO-HO-HO!!

We'll be the best pirate team the world has ever seen!

When Cliff and Polly got to pirate school,
anyone could see that they were, well . . .

different.

Cliff's heart sank. He did not want to be a failed pirate too.

AHOY!

In class, Cliff never sat still. There was too much to do!

Cliff tried very hard, but sometimes he messed up.

Like when he ate too many breakfasts . . .

or tied too many knots, which happened a lot.

To make matters worse, the sea was breezy.
And while Cliff tried to keep his singing to a hum,
Polly always joined in, so . . .

LOUDER!!

On the plus side, nobody, not even once,
asked if he had ants in his pants.

Because
I don't!

And nobody called him kooky.
But nobody called him clever either.

So, the night before report cards came out,
Cliff's timbers were shivering too much to sleep.

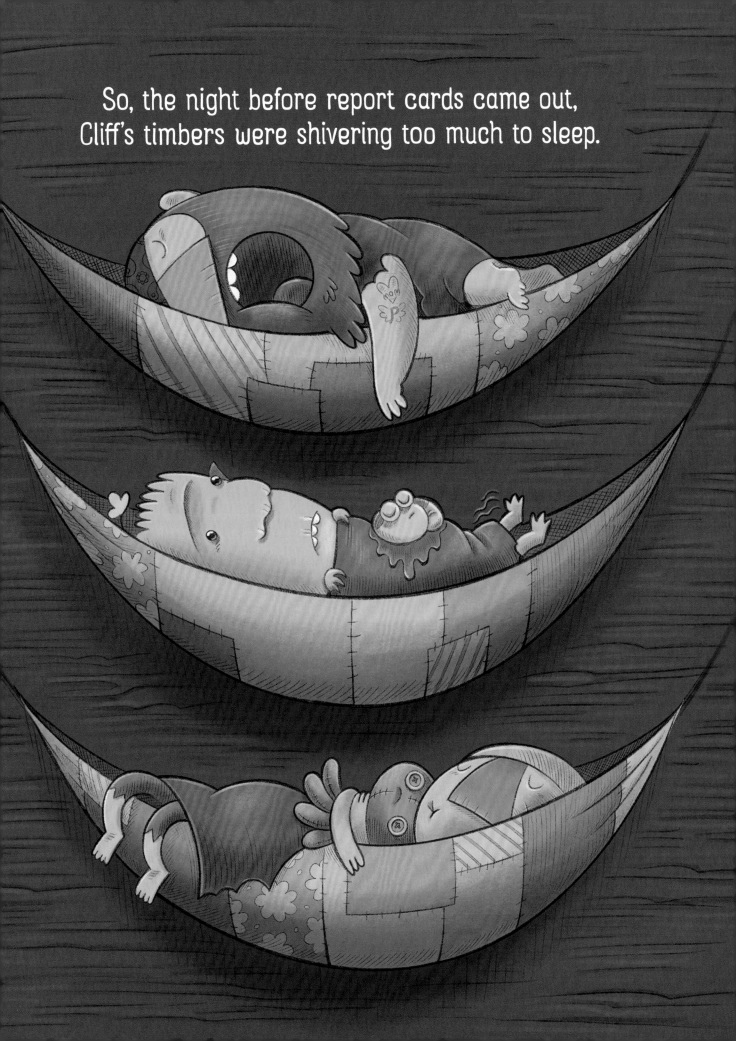

At first light, he found his
grades posted on the mast.

Cliff took one look and was
FLABBERGASTED!

CLIFF AND POLLY

 Sail Setting  **F**

 Treasure Tracking  **F**

 ARGH! Ability  **F**

He even got an **F** in Knot Know-How.

Because pirates are, well . . .

different.

For Ben, who never fails to be **F**ABULOUS!!!
. . . with a thousand thanks for giving me a chance.
—Barbara Davis-Pyles

For Jessica, Calvin, Vivian, Oliver, and Jovial.
—Justin Hillgrove

Manufactured in China by C&C Offset Printing Co. Ltd.
Shenzhen, Guangdong Province, in March 2020

LITTLE BIGFOOT with colophon is a registered
trademark of Penguin Random House LLC

24 23 22 21 20   9 8 7 6 5 4 3 2 1

Editors: Christy Cox, Ben Clanton
Production editor: Jill Saginario

ISBN: 978-1-63217-246-4

Library of Congress Cataloging-in-Publication Data
Names: Davis-Pyles, Barbara, author. | Hillgrove, Justin, 1976-
    illustrator.
Title: Cliff the failed troll : (warning: there be pirates in this book!) /
    Barbara Davis-Pyles ; illustrated by Justin Hillgrove.
Identifiers: LCCN 2019052872 | ISBN 9781632172464 (hardcover)
Subjects: CYAC: Ability--Fiction. | Individuality--Fiction. |
    Trolls--Fiction. | Pirates--Fiction. | Slugs (Mollusks)--Fiction.
Classification: LCC PZ7.1.D355 Cli 2020 | DDC [E]--dc23
LC record available at https://lccn.loc.gov/2019052872

Sasquatch Books
1904 Third Avenue, Suite 710
Seattle, WA 98101

SasquatchBooks.com

BARBARA DAVIS-PYLES is a first-rate fidgeter who sat still long enough to write *Grizzly Boy* and *Stubby the Fearfulless Squid*. She sings shanties and swashbuckles with words somewhere near the Salish Sea. Find out more at BarbaraDavisPyles.com.

JUSTIN HILLGROVE is a Pacific Northwest artist who loves painting monsters, robots, and other such nonsense, and he has worked on everything from comics and toys to tabletop games. Justin lives in Snohomish, Washington, with his wife, four kids, some chickens and ducks, a rabbit, and a dozen or so imaginary friends. Learn more at ImpsandMonsters.com.